Sam and Gram and the
First Day of School

Published by
MAGINATION PRESS
An Educational Publishing Foundation Book
American Psychological Association
750 First Street, NE
Washington, DC 20002

For more information about our books, including a complete catalog, please
write to us, call 1-800-374-2721, or visit our website at
www.maginationpress.com.

Editor: Darcie Conner Johnston
Art Director: Susan K. White
The text type is Cheltenham
Printed by Phoenix Color, Rockaway, New Jersey

Library of Congress Cataloging-in-Publication Data

Blomberg, Dianne L.
Sam and Gram and the first day of school / by Dianne L. Blomberg.
p.   cm.
Summary: Sam often feels frightened and lonely during his first day of
school, but when it is over, he eagerly tells his grandmother all about it.
ISBN 1-55798-562-6
[1. First day of school-Fiction. 2. Schools-Fiction. 3.Grandmothers-Fiction.]
I. Title. PZ7.B6199Sam   1999
[E]-dc21 98-31516
CIP
AC

Manufactured in the United States of America
10 9 8 7 6 5 4 3 2 1

To my husband, Ev, and to my children
and grandchildren. You are my inspiration
and remain my best work. -DLB

For my buddy, Kevin McElroy. -GU

Sam and Gram
and the
First Day of School

written by

Dianne Blomberg, Ph.D.

illustrated by

George Ulrich

MAGINATION PRESS • WASHINGTON, DC

On the first day of school, Sam walked to school with his Gram. In one hand he held his new blue backpack, and in the other he held Gram's hand tightly.

At school, Sam looked around at children
stepping off of school buses, at moms
and dads waving goodbye, and at
teachers greeting
children at the school
door. Sam looked up at Gram.

"Well, here we are," said Gram. "I think this is going to be a fun day. I'll
meet you right there by the flagpole at the end of the day." Sam wasn't
sure he wanted to let go of Gram's hand, but he did want to be brave like
the bigger boys and girls he saw. So he put his hand in his pocket,
where he kept his lucky seashell.

6

In the classroom, there were beautiful colors everywhere, and most things were just his size. The tables were small, the chairs were small, even the sink was small. But not everything was small. Sam's teacher, Mrs. Sarmiento, was big. She seemed bigger than anything in the room. Even her name was big.

Sam looked around the room at the other children. He thought about how much he missed his mommy, his daddy, and his dog, Atom. And he really missed his Gram. While Sam's mom and dad were at work each day, Gram took care of Sam. They played together, laughed together, ate lunch together, and talked about many things.

Sam felt sad, but he did not cry. He watched as Mrs. Sarmiento showed the children where to put their jackets and backpacks. He found out that he had his very own cubby where he could put his things every day. That made him feel good. Next, when Mrs. Sarmiento showed them all the paints and brushes in the art corner, Sam got excited. "I can't wait to paint a picture of Atom!" he said to himself.

But when Mrs. Sarmiento showed them the story circle, Sam started to miss his daddy, who always read him stories at bedtime. Sam decided that as soon as he got home from the first day of school, he would tell Gram about everything. Somehow Gram always made him feel better. He hoped she could help him feel better about school.

As Sam was thinking about Gram, Mrs. Sarmiento announced in her very big teacher voice, "Let's all get in line for play time. Stand side-by-side with a partner." Sam was scared. He had never done this before. He stood quietly, looking down at his shoes.

Mrs. Sarmiento walked down the line and showed each child how to stand side-by-side with a partner. Sam understood and did what she said. He remembered his dad and mom telling him he should listen to his teacher and follow directions.

Sam looked at the partner standing by his side. It was a girl with curly hair. Sam started to feel like there was a tiny smile inside of him. "Even my partner is the same size as I am," he thought.

Each child was wearing a sticky tag that had a name on it. Sam's tag was red and had three letters on it, an S, an A, and an M. That spelled Sam. Sam knew this because his mom had taught him a long time ago. Sam's partner had a sticky tag too. It was blue, but Sam could not read the name. It said, H-A-L-L-I-E. "What's your name?" Sam asked in a very quiet school voice. "My name is Hallie," said the curly-haired girl with the blue tag. Now Sam did not feel so scared. He walked next to Hallie all the way to the playground.

On the playground,
Sam slid down the twisty slide.

He dug in the sand pit.

He twirled on the tire swing.

15

Sam especially liked playing with Hallie. They both liked to jump over hills in the sand pit and run races. Sam decided to teach Hallie how to skip, just like Gram had taught him. "It's fun playing with Hallie," Sam thought, "she likes the same things that I do."

16

Soon it was time for Mrs. Sarmiento's class to return to their room. Sam and Hallie walked side-by-side in line. This time Sam did not look at his shoes. He looked at Hallie and smiled.

Mrs. Sarmiento told the children that she was going to teach them some interesting things about numbers. That made Sam think of Gram, because she had taught him many numbers. His favorite number was 6, just the same as Gram's. Sam started missing Gram again and wished he could go home.

When Mrs. Sarmiento said, "Who wants to hear about dinosaurs flying through outer space?" Sam's ears perked up. He forgot all about going home as he sat in the story circle listening to Mrs. Sarmiento read the adventures of Zippy Zach the astronaut and his super electron rocketship trip to Jupiter and Mars.

What was that? Did Sam hear Mrs. Sarmiento say it was time for lunch? Yes, Sam thought, he did! Sam smiled, and his stomach growled. Zach's adventures are exciting, but now Sam was hungry.

As he waited in the lunch line for his school pizza, he started to think about all of the lunches that he and Gram had eaten together.

Once they ate lunch with the monkeys at the zoo.

Once they ate lunch with the giant cactus at the garden in the park.

Sam sat at the table in the lunchroom and looked down at his school pizza, which he thought smelled funny. He also thought about those fun lunches with Gram, and felt himself getting sad again. But just then, he heard a quiet voice say, "Can we sit here?" Sam looked up and saw Hallie. She was standing next to a boy wearing a purple tag that said W-Y-A-T-T and a girl whose yellow tag said S-A-N-D-I. Sam smiled the biggest smile he could remember ever smiling and said, "YES!"

While Sam and Hallie and Wyatt and Sandi ate their pizza, they laughed about how funny it smelled. They talked about the tire swing and the twisty slide, and about Mrs. Sarmiento's big teacher voice, too. Hallie told Sam that her favorite number was 6. Before Sam knew it, it was time to take their pizza trays to the cafeteria helper and go back to Mrs. Sarmiento's classroom.

"It's time for art," announced Mrs. Sarmiento. "Yes!" whispered Sam, and he noticed that Mrs. Sarmiento's voice didn't seem so big now. While he made a picture of his dog Atom out of macaroni and Hallie painted a funny picture of her baby sister with purple skin, Mrs. Sarmiento explained to the class that music is art, too. She played a guitar and sang a song in Spanish called "La Cucaracha." It was about a bug! "Ugh!" said Wyatt, and Sam and Hallie giggled.

24

When it was time to go home, Mrs. Sarmiento told the children to get their things out of their cubby and stand in line with their partner. Sam and Hallie stood side-by-side as Mrs. Sarmiento led the class outdoors.

Sam and Hallie stopped walking side-by-side when Hallie got on the school bus. They waved goodbye and knew they would see each other tomorrow. Then Sam ran over to Gram, who was waiting by the flagpole to take him home from his first day of school.

At home, Gram and Atom had lemonade and pretzels waiting for Sam.

"What did you think of school today?" asked Gram. Sam remembered how much he had missed his family. Quietly, he took a sip of his lemonade. "I was scared," he finally said, "and I was sad, too. I missed all the fun stuff we do." Gram put her arm around Sam. "As you meet new friends and learn more about your school, things won't seem so scary and you won't feel so sad," she said gently.

That made Sam think about Hallie. Gram poured more lemonade, and Sam told her all about the curly-haired girl with the blue tag. He told her how they raced on the playground and laughed about Mrs. Sarmiento's big teacher voice. He told Gram how they ate lunch with Wyatt and Sandi, and they had so much fun they stopped thinking about the funny smell of the school pizza.

"Gram, you're right!" Sam jumped up. "After I met Hallie I didn't feel so sad!"

Atom got so excited and barked so loud they almost didn't hear the telephone ringing. It was Sam's mom. She wanted Sam to tell her all about the first day of school. "I just decided that I had a great day today!" he told her.

When Sam said goodbye to his mom, he hung
up the phone and threw his arms around Gram.
"I can hardly wait for tomorrow, Gram. I think I'm
really going to like the SECOND day of school!"

Things to Talk About

This story is intended to help your child think about all the feelings he or she may have about starting school—and to talk about them. Here are some suggested questions that you may ask your child after reading the story. By talking about Sam's first day at school, your child can begin to develop advance strategies for handling new feelings and situations that may occur at school.

How did Sam feel on his first day of school? Have you ever felt that way?
Where were you and what were you doing when you had these feelings?
What did you do to feel better?

Sam felt sad because he missed his family and his dog.
Have you ever missed someone you love? What did you do to help yourself feel better?

What happened when it was time for Sam to go outside and play at school, and Sam didn't know what to do?
Has anyone ever asked you to do something and you didn't know what to do or how to do it? What did you do?

What did Sam do when he met the curly-haired girl?
What do you do when you meet someone new?

What did Sam think when he discovered that Hallie liked the same things he did?
Have you ever met someone who likes some of the same things you like?
How did you feel about this person?

When Sam sat alone at the lunch table, how did he feel?
Have you ever felt the way Sam felt? What did you do to feel better?
Have you ever seen someone else feeling the way Sam felt?
Did you talk to that person? Did he (or she) feel better, like Sam?
How did that make you feel?

After school Sam told Gram that he sometimes felt sad and scared at school.
Do you remember what Gram told Sam?

Sam told Gram and his mom about the first day of school. This made Sam feel good.
When you are happy or sad or have something special to say, whom do you talk to?
How do you feel after you talk to this person?

Things to Do

Here is a handy list of things to do with your child during the weeks before school starts. The more familiar your new student is with the people, places, and procedures of the school day, the more comfortable and confident he or she will be when the time comes.

Visit the school playground with your child on an evening or weekend prior to the start of school. Play is a common activity that children use to become comfortable and familiar with their surroundings.

If your child will be riding a school bus, go for a ride together on a local bus. Compare the experience with the school bus ride as you are traveling. For example, you may say to your child, "You'll climb stairs just like this to get on the school bus, but you won't have to pay any money," "There will be a bus driver, just like on this bus, but your bus driver will say hello to you when you get on and will get to know your name," "You'll sit on a seat pretty much like this one and be able to look out the big window," and "The bus driver will tell you what to do and where to go if you don't know."

At this age, a child should always be accompanied by an adult. If you or another caregiver will be walking your child to school, the two of you should walk the complete route several times during the weeks prior to the first day of school so that you both are familiar with it. You may also take this time to reinforce safety issues regarding crossing streets, safety patrols, staying clear of the school bus, designated drop-off and pick-up areas, and so forth.

Schools are usually open a full week before opening day. If the school permits, visit the building with your child and tour the cafeteria, the bathrooms, the office, and your child's classroom. You may even find your child's teacher there for your child to meet.

Talk several times about what will happen when school lets out for the day. If your child is riding the bus, talk about who will be waiting at the bus stop at the end of the ride and where that will be. If you or someone else is picking up your child at school, talk about the procedure and the place for doing so. If you are a working parent, you may want to be home on the first, special day. If you can't, try to call your child soon after he or she gets home.

Encourage any older siblings to talk reassuringly about school—their feelings and experiences, as well as procedures—and to play the mentor to your child.

Before school starts, look for or create opportunities where your child can meet future classmates. Familiar faces on the first day of school can help alleviate a child's potential feelings of fear and loneliness.